Puffin Books
Editor: Kaye Webb

CANDY FLOSS

'I want that doll,' said horrid, spoilt Clementina
Davenport when she saw Candy Floss at the coconut
shy in her lovely pink gauze dress and her red shoes. But
people had wanted to buy Candy Floss before, and Jack,
who owned the coconut shy, always said 'Why, she's
my luck, couldn't sell that.'

But Clementina, with her twenty pairs of shoes and
her white piano, was much too spoilt to put up with
anything like *that*. If Jack wouldn't sell her the doll she
was going to get hold of her another way, even if it did
make Candy Floss so miserable she nearly cracked.

IMPUNITY JANE

'This little doll is very strongly made,' said the shop
woman. 'Why, you could drop her with impunity.' And
that was how Impunity Jane got her name.

She thought herself a dashing, swashbuckling sort of
doll, just right for narrow escapes riding in pockets on a
scooter or a swing, climbing trees or travelling in
aeroplanes, but instead she had to sit on a cold, hard
bead cushion in the dolls' house, quite still and very
bored. And it was a long tedious time before a boy called
Gideon rescued her.

No one understands dolls' feelings quite like Rumer
Godden, and the pint-sized sufferings of these two are
just as memorable as the tragedies of many far larger
heroines.

For readers of five and over.

Candy Floss

and

Impunity Jane

Rumer Godden

Illustrated by
Prudence Seward

Puffin Books

Puffin Books, Penguin Books Ltd,
Harmondsworth, Middlesex, England
Penguin Books Australia Ltd,
Ringwood, Victoria, Australia
Penguin Books Canada Ltd,
41 Steelcase Road West, Markham, Ontario, Canada
Penguin Books (N.Z.) Ltd,
182–190 Wairau Road, Auckland 10, New Zealand

Candy Floss first published by Macmillan 1960
Impunity Jane first published by Macmillan 1955
This edition published in Puffin Books 1975
Copyright © Macmillan 1955, 1960
Illustrations copyright © Prudence Seward, 1975

Made and printed in Great Britain by
Cox & Wyman Ltd, London, Reading and Fakenham
Set in Monotype Baskerville

Candy Floss

For Jane who thought of it

This is the tune Jack's music box played

Ah, my dear old   Au-gus-tine, Au-gus-tine, Au-gus-tine,

Ah, my dear old   Au-gus-tine,   ev - ery - thing's gone —

Mon-ey's gone, sweet-heart's gone—all is gone, Au-gus-tine,

Ah, my dear old   Au - gus - tine, ev - ery - thing's gone.

Once upon a time there was a doll who lived in a coconut shy.

You and I can say we live in London, or Chichester, or in Connecticut, France, Japan, Honolulu, or the country or town where we do live. She lived in a coconut shy.

A coconut shy is part of a fair. People come to it and pay their money to throw wooden balls at coconuts set up on posts. If anyone hits a coconut off the post he can keep it. It is quite difficult, but lots of nuts are won, and it is great fun.

This particular shy was kept by a young man called Jack.

There are many coconut shies in a fair, but Jack's was different. It had the same three-sided tent, the same red and white posts for the nuts, the same scar-

let box stands for the balls; it had the same flags and notices and Jack called out the same call: 'Three balls f'r threepence! Seven f'r a tanner!' (A tanner is what Jack called a sixpence.) All these were the same, but still this shy was different, for beside it, on a stool, Jack's dog sat up and begged by a little mechanical organ that Jack had found and mended till it played (he called it his music box). On top of the box was a little wooden horse, and as the music played – though it could play only one tune – the horse turned round and round and frisked up and down. On the horse's back sat a beautiful little doll.

The dog's name was Cocoa, the horse's name was Nuts, and the doll was Candy Floss.

A fair is noisy with music and shouting, with whistles and bangs and laughing and squeals as people go on the big wheel, the merry-go-rounds, or the bumper cars. Jack's music box had to play very loudly to be heard at all, but Cocoa, Nuts, and Candy Floss did not mind its noise; indeed, they liked it; no other shy had a music box, let alone a dog that begged, a horse that frisked, or a doll that turned round and round. A great many people came to Jack's shy to look at them – and stayed to buy balls and shy them at the nuts.

'We help Jack,' said Candy Floss, Cocoa, and Nuts.

Jack was thin and dark and young. He wore jeans, an old coat full of holes, and an old felt hat; in his ears were golden rings.

Cocoa was brown and tufty like a poodle; he wore

a collar for every day and a red, blue, and white bow for work. Cocoa's work was to guard the music box, Nuts, Candy Floss, and the old drawer where Jack kept the lolly (which was what he called money). Cocoa had also to sit on a stool and beg, but he could get down when he liked, and under the stool was a bowl marked 'Dog' and filled with clean water, so that he was quite comfortable.

Nuts was painted white with black spots; his neck was arched and he held his forelegs up. He had a black-painted mane and wore a red harness hung with bells.

Cocoa and Nuts were pretty, but prettiest of all was Candy Floss; she was made of china, with china cheeks and ears and nose, and she had a little china smile. Her eyes were glass, blue as bluebells; her hair was fine and gold, like spun toffee. She was dressed in a pink gauze skirt with a strip of gauze for a bodice. When she needed a new dress Jack would soak the old one off with hot water, fluff up a new one and stick it on with glue. On her feet were painted dancing shoes as red as bright red cherries.

The music box played:

Cocoa begged, Nuts frisked, Candy Floss turned round and round. All the children made their fathers and mothers stop to look. When they stopped, the fathers would buy balls and if anybody made a nut fall down Jack handed out a beautiful new coconut. He was kept very busy, calling out his call, picking up the balls; and the heap of pennies and sixpences in the lolly drawer grew bigger.

went the music box; Cocoa begged, Nuts frisked, and Candy Floss turned round and round.

When the coconuts were all gone Jack would empty the lolly drawer, put out the lights, and close the shy. He shut off the music box and let Cocoa get down. Nuts was covered over with an old red cloth so that he could sleep; Jack put Candy Floss into his pocket (there was a hole handy so that she could

see out) and, with Cocoa at his heels, went round the fair.

They went on the big merry-go-rounds where the big steam organs played 'Yankee Doodle' and 'Colonel Bogey' and other tunes. Jack sat on a horse or a wooden swan, a camel or an elephant, with Cocoa on the saddle in front of him and Candy Floss

safe in his pocket; round they went, helter-skelter, until Candy Floss was dizzy. The little merry-go-rounds had buses, engines, and motor-cars that were too small for Jack, but sometimes Candy Floss and Cocoa sat in a car by themselves. Here the music was nursery rhymes, and the children tooted the horns. Toot. Toot-toot-toot. Candy Floss wished she could toot a horn.

Sometimes they went to the Bingo booths and tried to win prizes. Once Jack had won a silk handkerchief, bright purple printed with shamrocks in emerald-green. Cocoa and Candy Floss thought it a most beautiful prize and Jack always wore it round his neck.

Sometimes they went on the bumper cars. When the cars bumped into one another the girls shut their eyes and squealed; Candy Floss's eyes would not shut, but she would have liked to squeal.

Best of all they went on the big wheel, with its seats that went up and up in the air high over the fair and the lights, so high that Candy Floss trembled, even though she was in Jack's pocket.

When they were hungry they would eat fair food. Sometimes they ate hot dogs from the hot-dog stall; Cocoa had one to himself but Candy Floss had the tip end of Jack's. Sometimes they had fish and chips at the fried-fish bar; Cocoa had whole fish and

Candy Floss had a chip. Often they had toffee apples; Cocoa used to get his stuck on his jaw and had to stand on his head to get it off. Sometimes they had ice-cream and Jack made a tiny cone out of a cigarette paper for Candy Floss.

When they were tired they came back to an old van that Jack had bought dirt cheap (which was what he called buying for very little money). He had mended it and now it would go anywhere. Jack put the music box and Nuts in the van too, so that they would all be together. Then he closed the doors and they all lay down to sleep.

Jack slept on the floor of the van on some sacks and an old sleeping-bag. Cocoa slept at Jack's feet. Candy Floss slept in the empty lolly drawer which Jack put beside his pillow; the sixpences and pennies had been put in a stocking that Jack kept in a secret place. He folded up the shamrock handkerchief to make the drawer soft for Candy Floss and tucked one end round her for a blanket.

As she lay in the drawer Candy Floss could feel Jack big and warm beside her; she could hear Cocoa breathing, and knew Nuts was under the cloth. Outside, the music of the fair went on; through the van window the stars looked like sixpences. Soon Candy Floss was fast asleep.

Fairs do not stay in one place very long, only a day, two days, perhaps a week. Then Jack would pack up the coconut shy, the lights and the flags, the posts, the nuts, the stands, and the wooden balls. He would take down the three-sided tent, put everything on the van, start it up, and drive away. The music box with Nuts travelled on the floor in front, Cocoa sat on the seat, but Candy Floss had the best place of all: Jack made the shamrock handkerchief into a sling for her and hung it on the driving mirror. Candy Floss could watch the road and see everywhere they went.

Sometimes the new fair was at a seaside town. Jack would stop the van and they would have a picnic on the beach. Cocoa would chase crabs, Nuts had some seaweed hay, and Jack found Candy Floss a shell for a plate.

Sometimes the fair was in the country and they

picnicked in a wood. Cocoa chased rabbits, not crabs, Nuts had moss for straw, and Jack found Candy Floss an acorn cup for a drinking bowl.

Sometimes they stopped in a field. Cocoa would have liked to chase sheep but he did not dare. Jack made daisy-chain reins for Nuts, Candy Floss had a wild rose for a hat; but no matter where they stopped to picnic, sooner or later the van would drive on to another fairground and Jack would put up the shy.

Cocoa would be brushed and his bow put on, and he would get up on his stool while Jack filled the bowl marked 'Dog'. The cloth came off the music box and Nuts would be polished with a rag until he shone. Then Jack would fluff up Candy Floss's dress and with his own comb spread out her hair. He washed her face (sometimes, I am sorry to say, with spit) and sat her carefully on the saddle and switched on the music and lights. 'Three f'r three-pence! Seven f'r a tanner!' Jack would cry.

went the music box; Cocoa begged, Nuts frisked, and Candy Floss turned round and round.

Sometimes the other fair people laughed at Jack about what they called his toys; but, 'Shut up out of that,' he would say. 'Toys? They're partners.' (Only he said 'pardners.')

'A doll for a partner? Garn!' they would jeer.

'Doll! She's my luck,' said Jack.

That was true. Jack's shy had more people and took in more pennies and sixpences than any other shy.

Cocoa, Nuts, and Candy Floss were proud to be Jack's partners; Candy Floss was very proud to be his luck.

Then one Easter they came to the heath high up above London which was the biggest fair of all (a heath is a big open space, covered with grass). Only the very best shies and merry-go-rounds, the biggest wheels were there. The Bingos had expensive prizes, there were a mouse circus, three rifle ranges, and stalls where you could smash china. There were toy-sellers and balloon-sellers, paper flowers and paper umbrellas. There were rows and rows of hot-dog stalls, fish bars, and toffee-apple shops.

Cocoa had a new bow. Nuts had new silver bells. Candy Floss had a new pink dress like a cloud. Jack painted the posts and bought a pile of new coconuts.

'Goin' to make more lolly'n ever we done,' said Jack. 'More sixpences'n stars in the sky.'

went the music box; and how well Cocoa begged, how gaily Nuts frisked, and Candy Floss turned round and round as gracefully as a dancer. More and more people began to come – Hundreds of people, thought Candy Floss. The wooden balls flew; pennies and sixpences poured into the lolly drawer.

'That's my luck!' cried Jack, and Candy Floss felt very proud.

Now not far from the heath, in a big house on the

hill leading down from the heath to the town, there lived a girl called Clementina Davenport.

She was seven years old, with brown hair cut in a fringe, brown eyes, a small straight nose, and a small red mouth. She would have been pretty if she had not looked so cross. She looked cross because she *was* cross. She said she had nothing to do.

'I don't know *what* to do with Clementina,' said her mother. 'What can I give her to make her happy?'

Clementina had a day nursery and a night nursery all to herself, and a garden to play in. She had a nurse who was not allowed to tell her to sit up or pay attention or eat her pudding or any of the other things you and I are told.

She had a dolls' house, a white piano, cupboards

full of toys, and two bookcases filled with books. She had a toy kitten in a basket, a toy poodle in another, and a real kitten and a real poodle as well. She had a cage of budgerigars and a pony to ride. Last Christmas her father gave her a pale blue bicycle, and her mother a watch, a painting box, and a painting book. Still Clementina had nothing to do.

'What *am* I to do with Clementina?' asked her mother, and she gave her a new television set and a pair of roller skates.

You might think Clementina had everything she wanted, but no, she was still quite good at wants and, on Easter Monday afternoon when the garden was full of daffodils and blossom, the sound of the fair came from the heath, over the wall, into the garden; and, 'I want to go to the fair,' said Clementina.

Another way in which Clementina was not like you or me was that for her 'I want' was the same as 'I shall.'

'*Not* a nasty common fair!' said her mother.

'I *want* to go,' said Clementina and stamped her foot, and so her father put on his hat, fetched his walking-stick, and took her to the fair.

Of course she went on everything: on the little merry-go-rounds where she rode on a bus and wanted to change to an engine, then changed to a car and back to the bus; on the big merry-go-rounds where she rode on a swan and changed to a camel and changed to a horse. She went on the bumper cars where she did not squeal but was angry when her car was hit; on the swing boats where she did not want to stop; and on the big wheel where she wanted to stop at once and shrieked so that they had to slow it and take her down. She cried at Bingo when she did not win a prize and screamed when the mice ran into the ring in the mouse circus. Her father bought her a toffee apple which she licked once and threw away, a balloon which she burst, and a paper umbrella with which she hit at people's legs.

Having everything you want can make you very tired. When Clementina was tired she whined. 'I don't like fairs,' whined Clementina, 'I want to go home.' (Only she said, 'I wa-ant to go ho-o-o-ome.')

'Come along then,' said her father.

'Fetch the car,' said Clementina, but motor-cars cannot go into fairs; and, 'I'm afraid you will have to walk,' said her father.

Clementina was getting ready to cry when she heard a gay loud sound:

and a call, 'Three f'r threepence! Seven f'r a tanner!' and she turned round and saw Candy Floss.

She saw Candy Floss sitting on Nuts, turning round and round as Nuts frisked up and down. Clementina saw the red shoes, the pink gauze, the way the blue eyes shone, the gold-spun hair, and, 'I want that doll,' said Clementina.

People often asked to buy Candy Floss, or Cocoa or Nuts; then Jack would laugh and say, 'You'll have to buy me as well. We're pardners,' and the people would laugh too, for they knew they could not buy Jack. 'Candy Floss? Why, she's my luck, couldn't sell that,' Jack would say. 'Pretty as a pi'ture, ain't she?' said Jack.

Now Clementina's father came to Jack. 'My little girl would like to buy your doll.'

'Sorry, sir,' said Jack. 'Not f'r sale.'

'I want her,' said Clementina.

'I will give you a pound,' said Clementina's father to Jack.

A pound is forty silver sixpences; but, 'Not f'r five hundred pounds,' said Jack.

'You see, Clementina,' said her father.

'Give him five hundred pounds,' said Clementina.

Her father walked away and Jack smiled at Clementina. 'I said *not* f'r five hundred pounds, little missy.'

I cannot tell you how furious was Clementina. She scowled at Jack (scowl means to make an ugly face). Jack stepped closer to Candy Floss and Cocoa growled; and, 'You cut along to yer pa,' said Jack to Clementina. Jack, of course, treated her as if she were any little girl, and she did not like that.

She made herself as tall as she could and said, 'Do you know who I am? I am Clementina Davenport.'

'And I'm Jack and these are Cocoa, Nuts, and Candy Floss,' said Jack.

'I am Clementina Davenport,' said Clementina scornfully. 'I live in a big house. I have a room full of toys and a pony. I have a bicycle and twenty pairs of shoes.'

'That's nice f'r you,' said Jack, 'but you can't have Candy Floss.'

I believe that was the first time anyone had ever said 'can't' to Clementina.

Jack thought he had settled it. In any case he was too busy picking up balls, taking in pennies and sixpences, handing out coconuts, and calling his call to pay much attention to Clementina. 'Cut off,' he told her, but Clementina did not cut off. She came nearer.

Cocoa, Nuts, and Candy Floss watched her out of the corners of their eyes.

Clementina was pretending not to be interested, but she came nearer still. If Candy Floss and Nuts had been breathing they would have held their breath.

Clementina came close and at that moment Cocoa got down to take a lap of water from his bowl. (It was not Cocoa's fault; he had never known a girl like Clementina.)

Nuts tried to turn faster, but he could only turn as fast as the music went. He wanted to kick, but he had to hold his forelegs up; he tried to shake his silver bells, but they did not make enough noise.

As Clementina's hand came out Candy Floss shrieked, 'Help! Help!' but a doll's shriek has no sound. She tried to cling like a burr to the saddle, but she was too small.

When Jack turned round Candy Floss had gone. There was no sign of Clementina.

When Clementina snatched Candy Floss, quick-as-a-cat-can-wink-its-eye she hid her in the paper umbrella and ran after her father.

Candy Floss was head-downward, which made her dizzy. The umbrella banged against Clementina's legs as she ran and that gave Candy Floss great bumps. She trembled with terror as she felt herself being carried far away; but she had not been brought up in a fair for nothing. She was used to being dizzy (on the merry-go-rounds), used to being bumped (on the bumper cars), used to trembling (on the big wheel), and when, in the big house on the hill, Clementina took her out of the umbrella Candy Floss looked almost as pretty and calm as she had on Nuts's saddle but china can be cold and hard; she made herself cold and hard in Clementina's hand and her eyes looked as if they were the brightest, clearest glass.

Dolls cannot talk aloud; they talk in wishes. You and I have often felt them wish and we know how

clear that can be, but Clementina had never played long enough with any of her dolls to feel a wish. She had never felt anything at all.

'But you will,' said Candy Floss, 'you will.'

Clementina turned all her dolls'-house dolls out of the dolls' house, higgledy-piggledy on to the floor. 'You will live in the doll's house,' she told Candy Floss.

'I live in a coconut shy,' said Candy Floss and her dress caught on the prim little chairs and tables and her hair caught on the shells that edged the scrap-pictures. Every time Clementina moved her she upset something. When she had knocked down a lamp, spilled a vase of flowers, and pulled the cloth off a table, Clementina took her out.

'Don't live in the dolls' house then,' said Clementina.

'You must wear another dress,' said Clementina and tried to take the pink one off, but she did not know, as Jack knew, how to soften the glue. All she did was to tear the gauze. Then she tried to put another dress over the top of the gauze skirt, but it stuck out and Candy Floss made her arms so stiff they would not go in the sleeves. Clementina lost patience and threw the dress on the floor.

She made a charming supper for Candy Floss: a daisy poached egg, some green grass spinach, and a blossom fruit salad with paint sauce. She had never taken such trouble over a supper before, but Candy Floss would not touch it.

'I eat hot dogs,' said Candy Floss, 'a chip, or a toffee apple.' Nor would she take any notice of the dolls' house's best blue and white china. 'I eat off a shell,' said Candy Floss. 'I drink from an acorn bowl.'

'Eat it up,' said Clementina, but Candy Floss tumbled slowly forward on to the supper and lay with her face in the blossom fruit salad.

'I shall put you to bed,' scolded Clementina and she got out the dolls'-house bed.

'I don't sleep in a bed,' said Candy Floss, 'I sleep in a lolly drawer,' and she made herself stiff so that her feet stuck out. When Clementina tucked them in, Candy Floss's head stuck out. Clementina put the bedclothes round her but they sprang up again at once. 'Are you trying to fight me?' asked Clementina.

Candy Floss did not answer, but the bedclothes sprang up again.

'Well, you can sit on a chair all night,' said Clementina and she took out a dolls'-house chair.

'I don't sit on a chair,' said Candy Floss, 'I sit on Nuts,' and as soon as Clementina put her on the chair she fell off.

'*Sit!*' said Clementina in a terrible voice, but a doll brought up in the noise and shouts of a fair is not to be frightened by a little girl's voice and Candy Floss did not blink an eye. 'Sit!' said Clementina and she sat Candy Floss hard on the chair. *Snap*, the chair legs broke.

Clementina stood looking at the pieces in her hand; she looked as if she were thinking. And if Candy Floss's little china mouth had not been smiling already, I should have said she smiled.

But she did not smile in the night. Clementina left her on the table when she went to bed and all night long Candy Floss lay on the cold table in that strange room.

There was no van; no music box with Nuts asleep under the old red cloth; no sound of Cocoa breathing; no Jack to feel big and warm; no lolly drawer to make a bed; no shamrock handkerchief. There was no music from the fair, no sixpence stars.

'And how can I get back?' asked Candy Floss. 'I *can't* get back. Oh, how will the shy go on? What will Jack do without his luck?' And all night the frightening words beat in her head: 'No luck. No luck. No Jack. No luck. No Nuts or Cocoa. No sixpences. No luck! No luck! No luck!'

Dolls cannot cry but they can feel. In the night Candy Floss felt so much she thought that she must crack.

Next morning it began again. Clementina took Candy Floss into the garden. 'You must go in my dolls'-house perambulator,' said Clementina.

'I go in a pocket,' said Candy Floss, and she would not fit in the perambulator. She held her head up so that it would not go under the hood and made her legs stiff so that they would not go in either. Clementina shook her until her eyes came loose in her head.

'You belong to me now,' said Clementina.

'I belong to Jack.'

Candy Floss, as we know, could not say these things aloud, but now Clementina was beginning to feel them. Clementina was not used to feeling; the more she felt, the angrier she grew, and she thought of something dreadful to say to Candy Floss. 'Pooh!' said Clementina. 'You're only a doll. The shops are full of dolls. Jack will have another doll by now. Do you think he wouldn't have bought another doll to take your place?'

Candy Floss seemed to sway in Clementina's hand. Another doll in her place! In all her places! On Nuts's back; in Jack's pocket; in the lolly drawer in the shamrock handkerchief. Another doll to be Jack's luck! What shall I do? thought Candy Floss. What can I do? And she cried out with such a big wish that she fell out of Clementina's hand on to the path and a crack ran down her back. 'Jack! Jack! Cocoa! Nuts! Help! Help! Help!' cried Candy Floss.

At that moment, in the fair, the merry-go-rounds started up.

All the merry-go-rounds up and down the heath began to play. The big wheel started and the rifles cracked in the rifle ranges. People began to cry 'Bingo!' and the toy-sellers and balloon-sellers started to shout. All the music in the fair began to play, louder and louder until it sounded as if the whole fair were in the garden.

Clementina picked Candy Floss up off the path and what had happened? Candy Floss was cracked; her eyes were loose, the shine had gone out of her hair, her face was covered with paint where she had fallen into the salad, and her dress was torn. As for its pink, you know how brown and dull pink spun sugar can go. Candy Floss's dress looked just like that.

'You're horrid,' said Clementina and she threw Candy Floss back on to the path.

The merry-go-round and the fair music seemed to say that too, 'You're horrid,' but they were saying it to Clementina.

'I think I shall go indoors and paint,' said Clementina. She went in but the fair music came into the house and now, as Clementina listened, she heard other things as well. 'She belongs to Jack.' 'You're horrid.' 'Cruel Clementina,' said the music.

'I won't sit still. I shall skip,' said Clementina, but though she skipped up to a hundred times she could not shut out that music. 'She belongs to Jack.' 'Cruel Clementina.' 'Poor Candy Floss;' and the big wheel turning – you could see the top of it from the garden – seemed to say, 'I can see. I see everything.'

When lunchtime came Clementina did not want any lunch. 'Are you ill?' asked her nurse and made Clementina lie down on her bed with a picture book. 'You look quite bad,' said the nurse.

'I don't!' shouted Clementina and hid under her blanket because that was what she did not want to feel, bad; but the bed and the picture book, even the blanket, could not shut out the fair, and the music never stopped: 'Bad Clementina.' 'Cruel Clemen-

tina.' 'She belongs to Jack.' 'Poor Candy Floss.'

Clementina put her head under the pillow.

Under the pillow she could not hear the music but she heard something else: thumpity-bump; thumpity-bump; it was her own heart beating. Clementina had not known she had a heart before; now it thumped just like the merry-go-round engine, and

what was it saying? 'Poor Candy Floss. Poor Candy Floss,' inside Clementina.

She lay very still. She was listening. Then she began to cry.

By and by Clementina sat up. She got out of bed and put on her shoes; then, just as she was, rumpled and crumpled from lying on the bed and tear-stained from crying, she tiptoed out of the room and went

43

down the stairs into the garden, where she picked up
Candy Floss and she tiptoed to the gate.

No one was about. She opened the gate and ran.

She ran up the hill to the heath and into the fair,
past the balloon-man and the toy-sellers, the fish-
and-chips bar, the hot-dog stands and the toffee-
apple stalls. She ran past the little merry-go-rounds
with the buses and cars, and the big merry-go-
rounds with the horses and swans, past the Bingos,

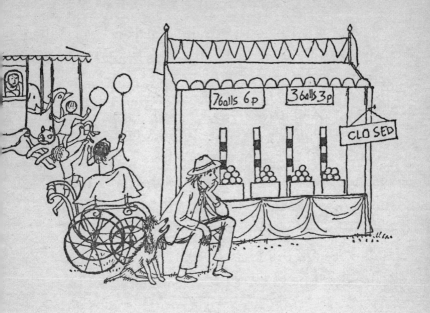

the mouse circus, the rifle ranges, and the big wheel
. . . and then she stopped.

The coconut shy was closed.

No lights shone; no coconuts were set up on the
red and white posts. The balls were stacked in their
scarlet stands. The music box was covered with the
old red cloth. Nuts could not be seen. Cocoa lay on
the ground with his head on his paws; now and
again he whimpered.

45

Jack was sitting on a box, hunched and still. When people came to the shy he shook his head. 'My luck's gone,' he said, and Cocoa put up his nose and howled.

Clementina had meant to put Candy Floss back on Nuts and then run away as fast as she could, but she could not bear it when she saw how miserable she had made them all. She could not bear to see Nuts covered up, Cocoa whimpering, Jack's sad face; and, without thinking or waiting, she cried, 'Oh *please*, don't be so sorry! I have brought her back.'

Jack stood up. Cocoa stood up. The cloth slithered off the music box and there was Nuts, standing up. 'Brought her *back*?' asked Jack, and Clementina forgot all about being Clementina Davenport in the big house on the hill; and, 'Yes, I'm Clementina. I took her,' she said and burst into tears.

When Jack saw what Clementina had done to Candy Floss he looked very, very grave and Cocoa growled; but Jack was used to mending things and in no time at all he had borrowed some china cement from the china-smashing stall and filled in the crack.

He would not let Clementina hold Candy Floss but he let her watch, though Cocoa still growled softly under his breath. Very gently he touched the loosened eyes with glue and made them firm again. He washed the torn skirt off and glued a fresh one on and cleaned the paint off Candy Floss's face; then he spun out her hair again and she looked as good as new. Cocoa stopped growling and Clementina actually smiled.

Then in a jiffy (which was what Jack called a moment) he put fresh coconuts on the posts and opened the ball stands. He put Cocoa's bow on and told him to jump on the stool; he ran over Nuts's paint with a rag so that it shone; then he put Candy Floss in the saddle and switched on the music box.

went the music box.

'Three balls f'r threepence! Seven f'r a tanner!' called Jack. His shout sounded so joyful, Cocoa begged so cleverly, Nuts frisked so happily, and

Candy Floss turned so gaily that the crowds flocked to the shy. 'Come'n help!' called Jack to Clementina and Clementina began to pick up the balls.

But who was this coming? It was Clementina's father and mother and with them the nurse and all the maids and a policeman, because there had been *such* a fuss when they had missed Clementina. They had searched all through the fair. Now they stopped at the coconut shy.

'Is *that* Clementina?' asked her father and mother, the nurse and the maids.

The cross look had gone from Clementina's face; she was too busy to be cross. Her cheeks were as pink as Candy Floss's dress; her eyes were shining as if they were made of glass; her hair looked almost gold.

'*Can* it be Clementina?' asked her father and mother, the nurse and the maids.

'Clementina, Clementina!' they called amazed.

'Three f'r threepence! Seven f'r a tanner!' yelled Clementina.

'What *am* I to do with her?' cried her mother.

It was the policeman who answered, the policeman who had been called out to look for Clementina. 'If I was you, mum,' said the policeman, 'I should leave her alone.'

Clementina was allowed to stay all afternoon at the shy. Her father and mother thought it was they who allowed her; Jack thought it was Jack. She worked so hard picking up balls that he gave her two

49

sixpences for herself, and Clementina was prouder of those sixpences than of all the pound notes in her money box (she calls it a lolly box now). 'I *earned* them,' said Clementina.

When her nurse came to take her home she had to say good-bye to Jack, Cocoa, Nuts, and Candy Floss; but, 'Not good-bye; so long,' said Jack.

'So long?' asked Clementina.

'So long as there's fairs we'll be back,' said Jack. 'Come'n look f'r us.'

When Clementina was in bed and happily asleep the fair went on.

went the music box.

'Three f'r threepence! Seven f'r a tanner!' called Jack. Cocoa begged, Nuts frisked and Candy Floss went round and round.

Impunity Jane

The Story of a Pocket Doll

For Richard Leigh Foster

'I'm Imp-imp-impunity Jane'

Once there was a little doll who belonged in a pocket. That was what *she* thought. Everyone else

thought she belonged in a doll's house. They put her in one but, as you will see, she ended up in a pocket.

She was four inches high and made of thick china; her arms and legs were joined to her with loops of strong wire; she had painted blue eyes, a red mouth, rosy cheeks, and painted shoes and socks; the shoes were brown, the socks white with blue edges. Her wig of yellow hair was stuck on with strong firm glue. She had no clothes, but written in the middle of her back with a pencil was:

$$5\tfrac{1}{2} d$$

This was in London, England, many years ago, when the streets were lit with gas and boys wore sailor suits and girls had many heavy petticoats. The little doll was in a toy shop. She sat on the counter near a skipping rope, a telescope, and a sailing ship; she was quite at home among these adventurous toys.

Into the toy shop came an old lady and a little girl.

'Grandma?' said the little girl.

'What is it, Effie?' asked the old lady.

'That little doll would just go in my doll's house!' said Effie.

'But I don't want to go in a doll's house,' said the

little doll. 'I want to be a skipping rope and dance out into the world, or a sailing ship and go to sea, or a telescope and see the stars!' But she was only a little fivepence-halfpenny doll and in a moment she was sold.

The shop woman was about to wrap her up when the old lady said, 'Don't put her in paper. She can go in my pocket.'

'Won't she hurt?' said Effie.

'This little doll is very strongly made,' said the shop woman. 'Why, you could drop her with impunity.'

'I know "imp",' said Effie. 'That's a naughty little magic person. But what is impunity?'

'Impunity means escaping without hurt,' said the old lady.

'That is what I am going to do forever and ever,' said the little doll, and she decided that it should be her name. 'Imp-imp-impunity,' she sang.

Effie called her Jane; afterwards, other children called her Ann or Polly or Belinda, but that did not matter; her name was Impunity Jane.

She went in Grandma's pocket.

Impunity Jane's eyes were so small that she could see through the weave of the pocket. As Effie and Grandma walked home, she saw the bright daylight and sun; she saw trees and grass and the people on the pavements; she saw horses trotting (in those days there were horse buses and carriages, not cars). 'Oh, I wish I were a little horse!' cried Impunity Jane.

It was twelve o'clock and the bells were chiming from the church steeples. Impunity Jane heard them, and bicycle bells as well. 'Oh, I wish I were a bell!' cried Impunity Jane.

In the park girls and boys were sending shuttle-cocks up into the air (in those days children played with shuttlecocks), and Impunity Jane wanted to be a shuttlecock flying up.

In the barracks a soldier was blowing a bugle; it sounded so brave and exciting that it seemed to ring right through her. 'A bugle, a horse, a bell, a shuttle-cock – oh, I want to be everything!' cried Impunity Jane.

But she was only a doll; she was taken out of

Grandma's pocket, put into Effie's doll's house, and made to sit on a bead cushion. Have you ever sat on a bead cushion? They are hard and cold, and, to a little doll, the beads are as big as pebbles.

There she sat. 'I want to go in a pocket, a pocket, a pocket,' wished Impunity Jane, but nobody heard.

Dolls, of course, cannot talk. They can only make wishes that some people can feel.

A doll's house by itself is just a thing, like a cup-

board full of china or a silent musical box; it can live only if it is used and played. Some children are not good at playing; Effie was one. She liked pressing flowers. She did not feel Impunity Jane wishing in the doll's house.

'I want to go out in a pocket,' wished Impunity Jane.

Effie did not feel a thing!

Presently Effie grew up, and another child, Eliza-

beth, had the doll's house. There were changes in the nursery; the old oil lamp and the candles were taken away, and there was gas light, like that in the streets. Elizabeth's nurse did not wear a high cap, as Effie's nurse had, and Elizabeth's dresses were shorter than Effie's had been; nor did she wear quite so many petticoats.

Elizabeth liked sewing doll clothes; she made clothes for Impunity Jane, but the stitches, to a little doll, were like carving knives. Elizabeth made a dress and a tiny muff. The dress was white with blue sprigs, the muff was cotton wool. Impunity Jane would have liked to have worn it as a hat; it could have been like that soldier's cap – and far off she seemed to hear the bugle – but, no, it was a muff. After she was dressed Elizabeth put her carefully back on the bead cushion.

Through the doll's house window Impunity Jane could see Elizabeth's brother playing with his clockwork railway under the table; round and round whirred the shining fast train. 'Oh! I wish I were a train,' said Impunity Jane.

The years went by; Elizabeth grew up and Ethel had the doll's house. Now the nursery (and the street outside) had electric lights, and there was an electric stove; the old high fender where Effie's and Elizabeth's socks and vests used to dry was taken away. Ethel did not have any petticoats at all, she wore a jersey and skirt and knickers to match.

Ethel liked lessons. She bought a school set with her pocket money, little doll books and a doll blackboard; she taught Impunity Jane reading and writing and arithmetic, and how to draw a thimble and a blackberry and how to sing a scale.

Through the open door Impunity Jane could see Ethel's brother run off down the stairs and take his hoop.

'Do re mi fa so la ti do,' sang Ethel.

'Fa! Fa!' said Impunity Jane.

After Ethel there was Ellen, who kept the doll's house shut.

Ellen wore grey flannel shorts and her curls were tied up in a pony tail. She went to a day school and, if her mother went out in the evening, she had a 'sitter'.

Ellen was too busy to play; she listened to the radio or stayed for hours in the living-room, looking at television.

Impunity Jane had now sat on the bead cushion for more than fifty years. 'Take me out,' she would

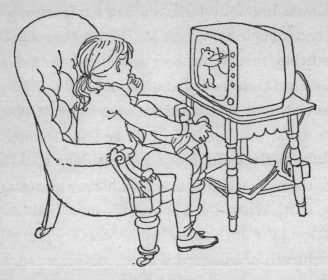

wish into Ellen as hard as she could. Impunity Jane
nearly cracked with wishing.

Ellen felt nothing at all.

Then one day Ellen's mother said, 'Ellen, you had
better get out all your toys. Your cousin Gideon is
coming to tea.'

Ellen pouted and was cross because she did not like
boys, and she had to open the doll's house and dust
its furniture and carpets. Everything was thick with

dust, even Impunity Jane. She had felt it settling on her, and it made her miserable. The clothes with the big stitches, the lessons, had been better than dust.

'Gideon! Gideon! What a silly name!' said Ellen.

To Impunity Jane it did not sound silly. 'G-G-G' – the sound was hard and gay, and she seemed to hear the bugle again, brave and exciting.

Gideon was a boy of seven with brown eyes and curly hair. When he laughed his nose had small wrinkles at the sides, and when he was very pleased – or frightened or ashamed – his cheeks grew red.

From the first moment he came into the nursery he was interested in the doll's house. 'Let me play with it,' he said, and he bent down and looked into the rooms.

'You can move the furniture about and put out the cups and saucers, as long as you put them all back,' said Ellen.

'*That*'s not playing!' said Gideon. 'Can't we put the doll's house up a tree?'

'A tree? Why the birds might nest in it!' said Ellen.

'Do you think they would?' asked Gideon, and he

laughed with pleasure. 'Think of robins and wrens sitting on the tables and chairs!'

Impunity Jane laughed too.

'Let's put it on a raft and float it on the river,' said Gideon.

'Don't be silly,' said Ellen. 'It might be swept away and go right out to sea.'

'Then fishes could come into it,' said Gideon.

'Fishes!'

Impunity Jane became excited, but Ellen still said, 'No.'

Gideon looked at Impunity Jane on the bead cushion. 'Does that little doll just sit there doing nothing?' he asked.

'What could she do?' asked Ellen.

Gideon did not answer, but he looked at Impunity Jane with his bright brown eyes; they twinkled, and suddenly Impunity Jane knew she could make Gideon feel. 'Rescue me,' wished Impunity Jane as hard as she could. 'Gideon, rescue me. Don't leave me here, here where Effie and Elizabeth and Ethel and Ellen have kept me so long. Gideon! *Gideon*!'

71

But Gideon was tired of Ellen and the nursery. 'I think I'll take a ball out into the garden,' he said.

'Gideon! Gideon, I shall crack!' cried Impunity Jane. 'G-I-D-E-O-N! G-I-D-E-O-N!'

Gideon stopped and looked at Impunity Jane; then he looked round at Ellen. Ellen was eating cherries from a plate her mother had brought in; she ought really to have shared them with Gideon, but she gobbled most of them up; now she was counting the stones. 'Tinker, tailor, soldier, sailor.' counted Ellen.

'Gideon, Gideon,' wished Impunity Jane.

'Rich man, poor man, beggar man' – and just as Ellen said, 'Thief,' Gideon, his cheeks red, slid his hand into the doll's house, picked up Impunity Jane, and put her into his pocket.

Ages and ages ago Impunity Jane had been in Grandma's pocket, but Grandma's pocket was nothing to Gideon's. To begin with, Gideon's pockets often had real holes in them, and Impunity Jane could put her head right through them into the world. Sometimes she had to hold on to the edges to avoid falling out altogether, but she was not afraid.

'I'm Imp-imp-impunity,' she sang.

Grandma had not run, and oh! the feeling of running, spinning through the air! Grandma had not

skated nor ridden on a scooter. 'I can skate and I can scoot,' said Impunity Jane.

Grandma had not swung; Gideon went on the swings in the park, and Impunity Jane went too, high and higher, high in the air.

Grandma had not climbed trees; Gideon climbed to the very top, and there he took Impunity Jane out

of his pocket and sat her on one of the boughs; she could see far over houses and steeples and trees, and feel the bough moving in the wind.

'I feel the wind. I feel the wind!' cried Impunity Jane.

In Grandma's pocket there had been only Impunity Jane and a folded white handkerchief that smelled of lavender water. In Gideon's pockets were all kinds of things. Impunity Jane never knew what she would find there – string and corks, sweets and sweet-papers, nuts, cigarette cards with beautiful pictures, an important message, a knife with a broken handle, some useful screws and tacks, a bit of pencil, and, for a long time, a little brown snail.

The snail had a polished brown shell with smoke-curl markings. Gideon used to take her out and put her down to eat on the grass; then a head with two horns like a little cow came out one side of the shell and a small curved tail at the other; the tail left a smeary silvery trail like glue; it made the inside of Gideon's pocket beautifully sticky. Gideon called the snail Ann Rushout because of the slow way she put out her horns.

'I once had a chestnut as a pretend snail,' said Gideon, 'but a real snail's much better.'

Impunity Jane thought so too.

But in all this happiness there was a worry. It worried Gideon, and so, of course, it worried Impunity Jane. (If dolls can make you feel, you make them feel as well.)

The worry was this. Gideon was a boy, and boys do not have dolls, not even in their pockets.

'They would call me "sissy",' said Gideon, and his cheeks grew red.

On the corner of the street a gang of boys used to meet; they met in the park as well. The leader of the gang was Joe McCallaghan. Joe McCallaghan had brown hair that was stiff as a brush, a turned-up nose, freckles, and grey eyes. He wore a green wolf cub jersey and a belt bristling with knives; he had every kind of knife, and he had bows and arrows, an air gun, a space helmet, and a bicycle with a dual brake control, a lamp, and a bell. He was nine years old and Gideon was only seven but, 'He quite likes me,' said Gideon.

Once Joe McCallaghan pulled a face at Gideon. 'Of course, I couldn't *think* of pulling one at him,' said Gideon. 'He knows me but I can't know him – yet.'

Once Gideon had a new catapult, and Joe McCallaghan took it into his hand to look at it. Gideon trembled while Joe McCallaghan stretched the catapult, twanged it, and handed it back. 'Decent weapon,' said Joe McCallaghan. Gideon would have said 'Jolly wizard!' But how ordinary that sounded now! 'Decent weapon, decent weapon,' said Gideon over and over again.

Impunity Jane heard him and her china seemed to grow cold. Suppose Joe McCallaghan, or one of the gang, should find out what Gideon had in his pocket?

'I should die,' said Gideon.

'But I don't look like a proper doll,' Impunity Jane tried to say.

That was true. The white dress with the sprigs had been so smeared by Ann Rushout that Gideon had taken it off and thrown it away. Impunity Jane no longer had dresses with stitches like knives; her dresses had no stitches at all. Gideon dressed her in a leaf, or some feathers, or a piece of rag; sometimes he buttoned the rag with a berry. If you can imagine a dirty little gypsy doll, that is how Impunity Jane looked now.

'I'm not a proper doll,' she pleaded, but Gideon did not hear.

'Gideon, will you mail this letter for me?' his mother asked one afternoon.

Gideon took the letter and ran downstairs and out into the street. Ann Rushout lay curled in her shell, but Impunity Jane put her head out through a brand-new hole. Gideon scuffed up the dust with the toes of his new shoes, and Impunity Jane admired the puffs and the rainbow specks of it in the sun (you look at dust in the sun), and so they came to the postbox.

Gideon stood on tiptoe, and had just posted the letter when – 'Hands up!' said Joe McCallaghan. He stepped out from behind the postbox, and the gang came from round the corner where they had been hiding.

Gideon was surrounded.

Impunity Jane could feel his heart beating in big jerks. She felt cold and stiff. Even Ann Rushout woke up and put out her two little horns.

'Search him,' said Joe McCallaghan to a boy called Puggy.

Impunity Jane slid quickly to the bottom of Gideon's pocket and lay there under Ann Rushout, the cork, the sweets, the pencil, and the string.

Puggy ran his hands over Gideon like a policeman

and then searched his pockets. The first thing he found was Ann Rushout. 'A snail. Ugh!' said Puggy and nearly dropped her.

'It's a beautiful snail,' said Joe McCallaghan, and the gang looked at Gideon with more respect.

Puggy bought out the cork, the sweets – Joe Mc-Callaghan tried one through the paper with his teeth and handed it back – the pencil, a lucky sixpence, the knife – 'Broken,' said Puggy scornfully, and Gideon grew red. Puggy brought out the string. Then Impunity Jane felt his fingers close round her, and out she came into the light of day.

Gideon's cheeks had been red; now they went dark, dark crimson. Impunity Jane lay stiffly as Puggy handed her to Joe McCallaghan; the berry she had been wearing broke off and rolled in the gutter.

'A doll!' said Joe McCallaghan in disgust.

'Sissy!' said Puggy. 'Sissy!'

'Sissy got a dolly,' the gang jeered and waited to see what Joe McCallaghan would do.

'You're a sissy,' said Joe McCallaghan to Gideon as if he were disappointed.

Impunity Jane lay stiffly in his hand. 'I'm Imp-imp-impunity,' she tried to sing, but no words came.

Then Gideon said something he did not know he could say. He did not know how he thought of it; it might have come out of the air, the sky, the pavement, but amazingly it came out of Gideon himself. 'I'm not a sissy,' said Gideon. 'She isn't a doll, she's a model. I use her in my model train.'

'A model?' said Joe McCallaghan and looked at Impunity Jane again.

'Will he throw me in the gutter like the berry?' thought Impunity Jane. 'Will he put me down and tread on me? Break me with his heel?'

'A model,' said Gideon firmly.

'She can be a fireman or a porter or a driver or a sailor,' he added.

'A sailor?' said Joe McCallaghan, and he looked at Impunity Jane again. 'I wonder if she would go in my model yacht,' he said. 'I had a lead sailor, but he fell overboard.'

'She wouldn't fall overboard,' said Gideon.

Joe McCallaghan looked at her again. 'Mind if I take her to the pond?' he said over his shoulder to Gideon.

Now began such a life for Impunity Jane. She, a little pocket doll, was one of a gang of boys! Because of her, Gideon, her Gideon, was allowed to be in the gang too. 'It's only fair,' said Joe McCallaghan, whom we can now call Joe, 'it's only fair, if we use her, to let him in.'

Can you imagine how it feels, if you are a little doll, to sit on the deck of a yacht and go splashing across a pond? You are sent off with a hard push among ducks as big as icebergs, over ripples as big as waves.

Most people would have been afraid and fallen overboard, like the lead sailor, but, 'Imp-imp-impunity,' sang Impunity Jane and reached the far side wet but perfectly safe.

She went up in aeroplanes. Once she was nearly lost when she was tied to a balloon; she might have floated over to France, but Gideon and Joe ran and

ran, and at last they caught her in a garden square, where they had to climb the railings and were caught themselves by an old lady, who said she would complain to the police. When they explained that Impunity Jane was being carried off to France the old lady understood and let them off.

The gang used Impunity Jane for many things: she lived in igloos and wigwams, ranch-houses, forts

and rocket ships. Once she was put on a Catherine Wheel until Joe thought her hair might catch fire and took her off, but she saw the lovely bright fire-

works go blazing round in a shower of bangs and sparks.

She was with Joe and Gideon when they ran away to sea, and with them when they came back again because it was time for dinner. 'Better wait till after Christmas,' said Joe. Gideon agreed – he was getting a bicycle for Christmas – but Impunity Jane was sorry; she wanted to see the sea.

Next day she was happy again because they started digging a hole through to Australia, and she wanted to see Australia. When they pretended the hole was a gold mine, she was happy to see the gold, and when the gold mine was a cave and they wanted a fossilized mouse, she was ready to be a fossilized mouse.

'I say, will you sell her?' Joe asked Gideon.

Gideon shook his head, though it made him red to do it. 'You can borrow her when you want to,' he said: 'But she's mine.'

But Impunity Jane was not Gideon's, she was Ellen's.

The gang was a very honourable gang. 'One finger

wet, one finger dry,' they said, and drew them across their throats; that meant they would not tell a lie. Gideon knew that even without fingers they would never steal, and he, Gideon, had stolen Impunity Jane.

She and Gideon remembered what Ellen had said as she counted cherrystones (do you remember?). 'Rich man, poor man, beggar man, thief,' said Ellen.

'Thief! Thief!'

Sometimes, to Gideon, Impunity Jane felt as heavy as lead in his pocket; sometimes Impunity Jane felt as heavy and cold as lead herself. 'I'm a thief!' said Gideon and grew red.

Impunity Jane could not bear Gideon to be unhappy. All night she lay awake in his pyjama pocket. 'What shall I do?' asked Impunity Jane. She asked Ann Rushout. Ann Rushout said nothing, but in the end the answer came. Perhaps it came out of the night, or Ann's shell, or out of Gideon's pocket, or even out of Impunity Jane herself. The answer was very cruel. It said, 'You must wish Gideon to put you back.'

'Back? In the doll's house?' said Impunity Jane. 'Back, with Ellen, Ellen who kept it shut?' And she said slowly, 'Ellen was worse than Ethel or Elizabeth or Effie. I can't go back,' said Impunity Jane, 'I can't!' But, from far off, she seemed to hear the bugle telling her to be brave, and she knew she must wish, 'Gideon, put me back.'

She wanted to say, 'Gideon, hold me tightly,' but she said, 'Gideon, put me back.'

So Gideon went back to Ellen's house with Impunity Jane in his pocket. He meant to edge round the nursery door while his mother talked to Ellen's mother, then open the doll's house and slip Impunity Jane inside and on to the bead cushion. He went upstairs, opened the nursery door, and took Impunity Jane in his hand.

It was the last minute. 'No more pockets,' said Impunity Jane. 'No more running and skating and swinging in the air. No more igloos and ripples. No rags and berries for frocks. No more Ann Rushout. No more warm dirty fingers. No more feeling the wind. No more Joe, no gang, not even Puggy. No more ... Gideon!' cried Impunity Jane – and she cracked.

But what was happening in Ellen's nursery? The doll's house was not in its place – it was on the table with a great many other toys, and there was Ellen sorting them and doing them up in parcels.

'I'm going to give all my toys away,' said Ellen with a toss of her head. 'I'm too old to play with them any more. 'I'm going to boarding-school. Wouldn't you like to go to boarding-school?' she said to Gideon.

'No,' said Gideon.

'Of course, you're still a *little* boy,' said Ellen. 'You still like toys.'

'Yes,' said Gideon, and his fingers tightened on Impunity Jane.

'Would you like a toy?' asked Ellen who was polishing a musical box.

'Yes,' said Gideon.

'What would you like?' asked Ellen.

'Please,' said Gideon. His cheeks were bright red. 'Please' – and he gulped – 'could I have' – gulp – 'the pocket doll' – gulp – 'from the doll's house?'

'Take her,' said Ellen without looking up.

Gideon has a bicycle now. Impunity Jane rides on it with him. Sometimes she is tied to the handle-bars, but sometimes Gideon keeps her where she likes to be best of all, in his pocket. Now Impunity Jane is not only his model, she is his mascot, which means she brings him luck.

The crack was mended with china cement by Gideon's mother.

Ellen went to boarding-school.

As for the doll's house, it was given away.

As for the bead cushion, it was lost.

About the Author

Rumer Godden, novelist, playwright and poet, was born in 1907 in Sussex and spent the early years of her childhood in India. When she was twelve, she and her three sisters were sent to school in England, but later she went back to India and has been going backward and forward ever since, perpetually homesick for one or the other.

Distinguished for the exceptionally wide range of her writing, Miss Godden has achieved great success in the field of children's books. These are about small things – dolls, mice, and little girls, and in such charming and delicate stories as *The Dolls' House*, *Miss Happiness and Miss Flower*, *Little Plum*, *The Story of Holly and Ivy* (all published in Puffins) *The Mousewife*, *Mouse House*, *The Kitchen Madonna* and *Operation Sippacik*, she has established a reputation as one of the leading authors writing today for children. Her translations from the French of Carmen Bernos de Gasztold's enchanting *Prayers from the Ark* appeared in 1963, followed by a further volume, *The Beast's Choir*, in 1967.

Miss Godden now lives in Rye, Sussex, in a house which once belonged to Henry James.

The Diddakoi was recently published in Puffins.